For my parents

© 2004 l'école des loisirs, Paris as *Bonne Nuit, Ma Cocotte*

This edition published in 2011 by
Eerdmans Books for Young Readers,
an imprint of William B. Eerdmans Publishing Co.
2140 Oak Industrial Dr. NE, Grand Rapids, Michigan 49505
P.O. Box 163, Cambridge CB3 9PU U.K.

www.eerdmans.com/youngreaders

11 12 13 14 15 16 17   10 9 8 7 6 5 4 3 2 1

Manufactured at Tien Wah Press in Singapore, August 2010, first printing

Library of Congress Cataloging-in-Publication Data

Jadoul, Émile.
[Bonne nuit, ma coquette. English]
Good night, Chickie / by Émile Jadoul.
p. cm.
Summary: Mother Hen reassures Chickie, and Chickie's bunny, that she is nearby and keeping watch over them at bedtime.
ISBN 978-0-8028-5378-3 (alk. paper)
[1. Bedtime — Fiction. 2. Parent and child — Fiction. 3. Chickens — Fiction.] I. Title.
PZ7.J153195Goo 2011
[E] — dc22
2010024985

Émile Jadoul

Good Night, Chickie

Eerdmans Books for Young Readers

Grand Rapids, Michigan • Cambridge, U.K.

Every evening,
Mother Hen puts
Chickie to bed.

Good night, Chickie, sweet dreams!

Good night, Mother Hen!

You're wearing your pretty necklace!
Are you going out, Mother Hen?
You're not going out, are you?

No, no, Chickie,
I'm not going out.
Good night!

You see, Bunny,
Mother Hen has her pretty
necklace on just to look nice.
She's not going out.
There's no need to be afraid!

Mother Hen! Mother Hen!
Are you there?
Bunny can't hear you.

Yes, I'm here, Chickie.
I'm in the kitchen.
Don't worry.
Go to sleep now.

Mother Hen! Mother Hen!
Are you there?
Bunny needs to go to the bathroom.

I'm here, Chickie, in the living room.
Go to the bathroom and then get back in bed!

Mother Hen! Mother Hen!
Are you there?
What's that noise?
Bunny is really scared . . .

Yes, Chickie, I'm here.
It's just the wind blowing . . .

. . . close your eyes now.

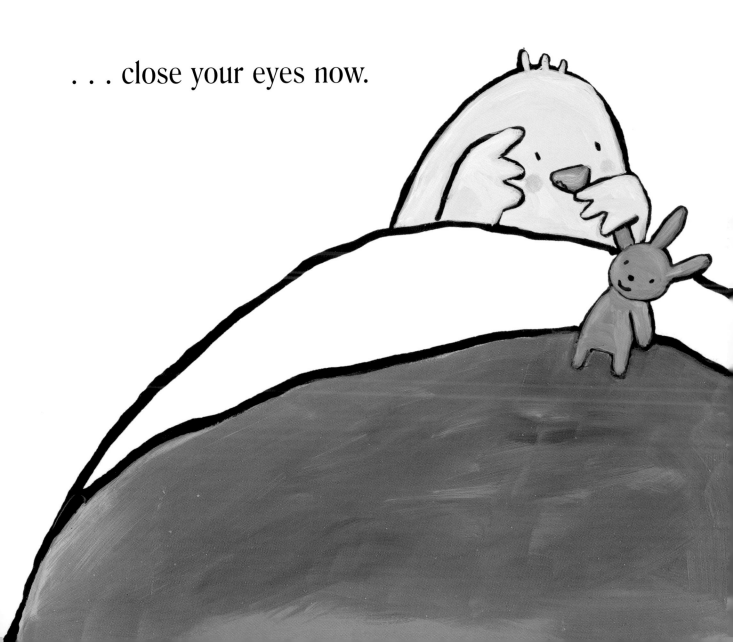

Mother Hen! Mother Hen!
Are you there?
Bunny is scared of the dark!

Yes, Chickie, I'm here!
Turn your bedside lamp on
and go back to bed!

Mother Hen! Mother Hen!
Are you there?
Bunny wants one last kiss . . .

. . . and so do I!

One last kiss then!
Good night, Chickie!

Good night, Mother Hen!

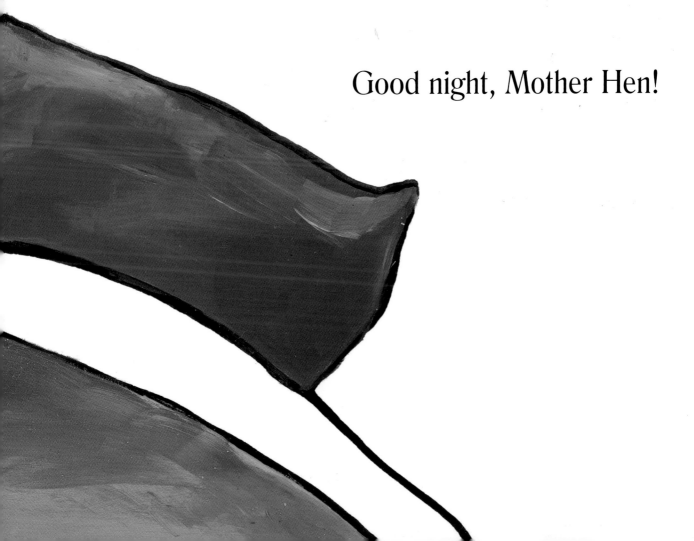

You see, Bunny,
Mother Hen is there.
So stop worrying.
Let me sleep now!